Springer's Journey

Naomi Black

Virginia Heaven

Written by Naomi Black
Illustrations by Virginia Heaven

SAN JUAN
PUBLISHING

SAN JUAN PUBLISHING
P.O. Box 923
Woodinville, WA 98072
425-485-2813
sanjuanbooks@yahoo.com

Publisher: Michael D. McCloskey
Design & Production: Megan Dew, Two Dogs Long, LLC

ISBN 0-9707399-3-1
Library of Congress Catalog Card Number: 2006902256

First Printing 2006
10 9 8 7 6 5 4 3 2 1
Printed in United States of America

To my fellow kayakers
and
For Mike

In the cold, cold waters of the Pacific Ocean …

... in the deep kelp forest, among the silly sea otters ...

... a young Orca whale named Springer lived with her family pod.

Springer spent her days splashing and swimming with her mother and diving far down into the deep kelp forest, looking for tasty salmon to eat.

One day, Springer's mother got very sick.

Springer tried to help her, but nothing made her better. She just got more and more sick.

On a bright and sunny winter morning, Springer's mother died.

Springer missed her mother every day, and she was very, very sad.

She wished she could have done something to make her mother better.

Since she now had no mother to take care of her, Springer's aunts and uncles and cousins all watched over the young Orca.

But even though Springer loved her family pod, none of them was her mother.

Springer visited the kelp forest often, for it reminded her of her mother.
But each time she swam farther and farther away from her family.

One day, she swam so far away that she
couldn't find her way back.

She asked the eight-armed octopus for help ...

She asked the thick-lipped cod for help ...

She asked the sleek-spotted seal for help,

but no one knew the way home.

She even asked the sea otters, but sea otters are silly. They just kept on playing with their prickly sea urchin dinners.

So Springer swam off to find her own way home.

She swam for days and days, all alone,

past reefs and islands,

through channels and inlets,

through deep, swift water

until she came to a place that was noisy and strange.

By now it was winter. Springer was tired and she didn't feel very well.
There were lots of boats and lots of people, but not many salmon to eat.
Springer grew very hungry.

She didn't know where to go, and she missed her mother so very much.

One day a boat rowed up to her.  Springer asked the boat if it knew the way back to the kelp forest, but it didn't.

She asked another boat,

then another,

then another.

Soon there were lots of boats, and Springer thought that one of them must know the way home, so she asked them every day.

But none of the boats knew.

Springer got more and more lonely

and more and more hungry.

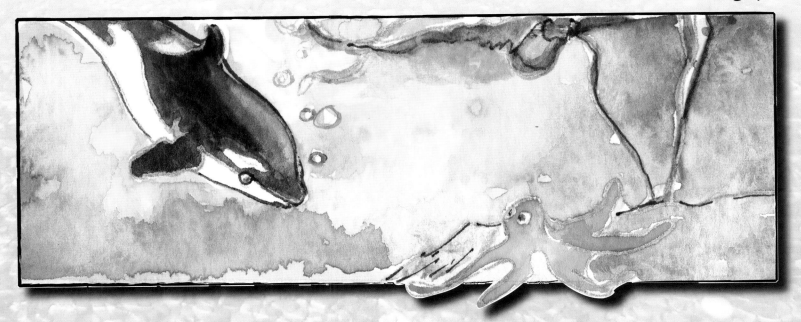

One afternoon, she set off to see the giant
old ferryboat that slowly chugged its way
back and forth across the water.

She asked the wise old ferryboat if it knew the way to the kelp forest. Its big hinges creaked and groaned as it told her that the journey was far too long for a little Orca whale such as herself.

Springer told the ferryboat about how much she missed her mother. She asked it to be her mother so she wouldn't be so lonely. She decided to stay with the ferryboat and learn to be a boat instead of an Orca whale.

Springer swam back and forth with the ferry every day, learning schedules and routes and other things that ferryboats know.

But the ferryboat didn't eat salmon as Springer did, and even though Springer was a little less lonely, she was still very, very hungry.

The winter passed, and the spring sun warmed the water.
On a bright, cool morning, some small boats came to visit her and the old ferry.
They said to Springer that all the boats had told her story to other boats …

… who had
told it to other
boats …

… who had
told it to
other boats.

So everyone for miles and miles around knew about Springer, and everyone wanted to help her find her way home. Springer told the boats she was learning to be a ferry. She couldn't go home.

But the wise old ferryboat knew that whales can't be ferries, no matter how hard they try.
She knew Springer had to find her way back to the kelp forest
where her family pod lived.

So Springer went off with the little boats to a floating pen near some docks.

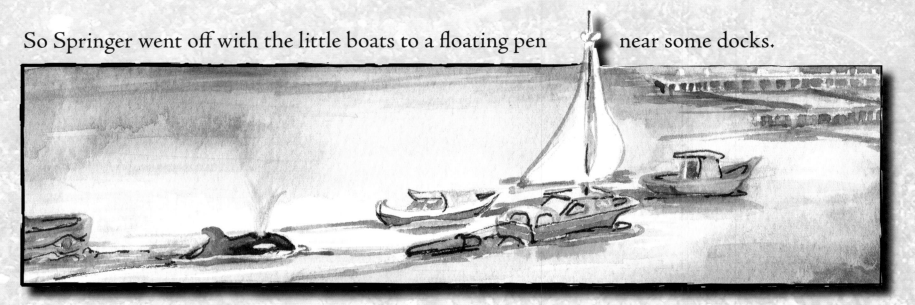

Springer was tired and sick and hungry because she hadn't eaten the ferryboat food or slept in the ferryboat beds.

At the docks, many busy people did all sorts of busy people things. They weighed her in a big sling, they gave her medicine to help her feel better, and they petted her so she wouldn't feel so lonely.

Springer talked to the people all the time, but they spoke in funny, tiny voices that she couldn't understand.

Springer found lots of tasty salmon in the pen, so she ate …

… and ate …

… and ate …

… until her belly was full and round.

A few weeks passed, and Springer started  to feel better.

She wasn't as hungry anymore, and she wasn't as sick.

She thought more and more about home and how much she missed the kelp forest with its silly sea otters and the rest of her family pod.

One morning when the summer sun rose very early and the water was warm, a huge boat came to Springer's pen. It told her that a way back to the kelp forest had been found.

It was there to take Springer home.

The people put her in a big sling and raised her far, far above the water.

Then they put her in a little tank just her size on the deck of the boat.

The people kept cold water running in her little tank to keep her cool, and they stayed with her so she wouldn't be scared.

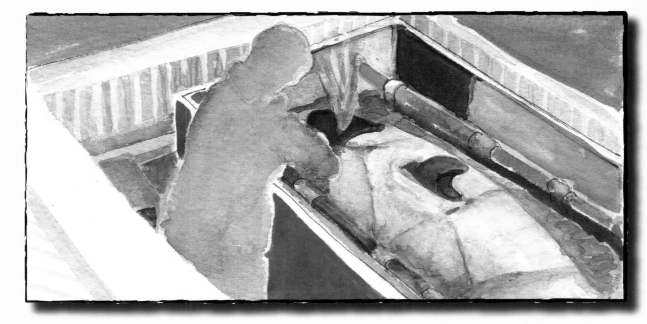

Springer talked to the
people as the boat traveled
on its long journey.

She told the people
about her home.
She told them stories about
the eight-armed octopus and
the thick-lipped cod.
She told them about her
family and the tasty salmon
she liked.

Most of all, she told
them how happy she was
to be going home.

That afternoon, Springer started to get very hot, because her little tank was too small to let her dive down into the water. She told the people she was getting too hot, so they put ice in her tank to make her feel better.

That evening the people took Springer to a little inlet with a floating pen in the cold, cold water.

She swam happily around in the cool sunset and found lots of tasty salmon to eat.

As dusk fell, she heard a faraway noise. Springer became very quiet and listened very, very hard.

She called out, and she heard a reply. It was her grandmother! Her grandmother was swimming by the inlet! She was home!

Springer could hardly wait until she could go back to the kelp forest.
She waited all night long, talking to her grandmother from her pen until dawn.

As the morning's rays shimmered off the water, the floating nets were lowered.

Springer said goodbye to the people, and she swam excitedly off to see her family.

She was so happy to see her grandmother and the rest of her family that she swam and splashed and turned round and round in the water. Springer squealed and squeaked and clicked in her Orca voice,

telling everyone she was home! She was home!

Her grandmother was very serious. She told Springer that her mother had loved her very much, and that Springer should never forget her, but all the Orcas in the family pod would take care of her now.

Springer knew that her mother was gone. She understood that her grandmother couldn't bring her mother back.

Springer thought about her adventure. She thought about how hard it was to be a ferryboat and how tired and sick she had gotten.

She thought about how happy she was to see her grandmother again and how much she missed the kelp forest.

Now Springer and her grandmother and aunts and uncles and cousins and nieces and nephews and the rest of her family pod swim and dive together in the cold, cold waters of the Pacific Ocean, in the deep kelp forest, among the silly sea otters.

Springer thinks of her mother sometimes.
She still misses her, but she knows that she has a family that loves her very much.
And she loves them too.

Afterword

This book is based on a true story. In it, we have been introduced to Springer, the orphaned orca. Far from family and home waters, Springer's lonely, solitary journey by chance brought her near to Seattle, Washington in 2002, and in doing so she found her way into our hearts.

We will never know the circumstances surrounding the death of Springer's young mother, Sutlej, nor the reasons why Springer became separated from her community. Knowing that orcas, like Springer, normally spend their entire lives with their mother, family and community, we can only imagine how frightened the 1½ year old baby Springer felt, alone and drifting on unfamiliar currents. Even though this strange journey had a toll on the little orca, something within her made her hold on, and she survived long enough for concern for her plight to turn into action.

Little Springer taught us all a valuable lesson in trust. Trust that it was all right for people to sometimes intervene and cross the invisible boundary that so often separates us from the wild world. Trust that all the knowledge from years of scientific research could find where she belonged. And perhaps above all, trust that all of us, whether scientists, government officials, non-governmental organizations, or the public can solve problems if we resolve to work together.

For those of us concerned about the well being of whales, the oceans and our fragile planet, Springer's story will remain an inspiration for years to come.

Helena Symonds & Dr. Paul Spong
Whale Research Directors
OrcaLab, British Columbia, Canada

October 2005

Interesting Websites and Online Information

Springer's Journey, San Juan Publishing:
www.springersjourney.com

Learn more about Orca Research and the Kelp Forest:
www.orcalab.org

See life in the Kelp Forest live!
www.orca-live.net

Information about Springer and her family:
www.orcanetwork.org

The Pacific Coast and its Marine Wildlife
Vancouver Aquarium: www.vanaqua.org
Fisheries and Oceans Canada: www.pac.dfo-mpo.gc.ca
National Parks Conservation Organization: www.npca.org
Friday Harbor Whale Museum: www.whalemuseum.org
The Center for Whale Research: www.whaleresearch.com

Environmental, Conservation and Stewardship Groups:
Project Sea Wolf: www.home.earthlink.net/~projseawolf
Born Free: www.bornfree.org.uk
Earth Island Institute: www.earthisland.org
Organisation Cetacea: www.orcaweb.org.uk

Catamaran "Catalina" (Springer's ride home):

With Gratitude...

We would like to thank all of the people who helped make this book possible: Mike McCloskey, Seattle Preparatory School, Gary and Linda Heinen, Bob Hartnett, Paul Spong & Helena Symonds, Matt Nichols at Nichols Brothers Boat Builders and Sue Massey. Without your help, support, dedication, optimism, criticism, energy, passion and belief, this book would not have been possible. Thank you.

About the Author & Illustrator

The text is written by Naomi Black, Computer Geek and Orator. A native Seattleite, Naomi grew up in the Pacific Northwest, often finding herself in the wilderness and on the sea. This is her first book.

Illustrations are the work of Virginia Heaven, an artist and former art teacher at Seattle Preparatory School. Virginia has traveled the Northwest coast by kayak as far north as the Queen Charlotte Islands. Johnstone Strait and the surrounding area are familiar territory to her, and her love of the wilderness and its creatures are apparent in the spirit of the illustrations.